The Ha

Shåne Maløney Guy Ruñdle

The Happy
Phrase

EVERYDAY CONVERSATION MADE EASILY

TEXT PUBLISHING MELBOURNE AUSTRALIA

The Text Publishing Company
Swann House
22 William Street
Melbourne Victoria 3000
Australia
www.textpublishing.com.au

This edition published 2004

Printed and bound by Griffin Press
Typeset by J&M Typesetting
Page design by Chong Wengho
All illustrations by Bill Wood Illustrations,
except for those that aren't.

National Library of Australia
Cataloguing-in-Publication data:

Maloney, Shane.
The happy phrase : everyday conversation made easily.
ISBN 1 920885 46 3.

1. Conversation - Miscellanea. 2. English language - Terms and phrases. 3. Social skills. I. Rundle, Guy. II. Title.

302.346

To A,

FOR MANY HAPPY PHASES.

— GR

THANKS TO PHRASES GALORE
(FORMERLY CLAUSES 'R' US) FOR
THE GENEROUS DISCOUNT.

— SM

Why this book?

How often have you been embarrassed by your lack of quick wittedness in spoken conversation? Often, we bet.

You are not alone. It happens to one and all, whether native speaker or otherwise. English is one slippery motherfucker, after all.

This book aims to correct that deficiency by placing hundreds of felicitous phrases at your disposal. Harmonious to the ear and pleasing to the eye, these happy phrases have been selected by our team of experts for their ease of memorisation. Simply commit them to heart and you will always have just the right phrase at your fingertips for any social or professional interaction.

Who for this book?

For you! For them! For us! For all bent on improving one's good self.

Perchance you began to speak English at your birth. Mayhap you apprehended it first behind some foreigner's school desk. However learned, you grasp it well. Your fluency is good. Your accent is permeable. Your vocabulary is copiously ample. Your idiom is ticketty-boo.

But still, you feel a lack of facility. You wish more in repartee to excel. You desire the quick quip and the ready saw, dependent on the situation.

Be you a public figure or an insignificant nobody, *The Happy Phrase* is imprinted with you in mind. Alone of suchlike books, it will furnish you with a multitude of conversational gambits, ready retorts and charming courtesies for any, each and all circumstances wherein you may find yourself in intercourse with fellow Anglophones.

How to this book?

The Happy Phrase organises its bulk into three easy-to-grip bits.

Our 327 Indispensable Phrases:

These should be fixed in the head. Say them aloud with many repetitions. Then again repeat them over and over. Practice with diligence and they will be tripping from your tongue. Soon you will be ready to find them employment in cases of dialogue.

Our Reasonably Interesting Facts:

These little-known snippets of language lore will amuse and scintillate you with fluency-enhancing particulars and examples.

Our Handy Tips:

Mindful of the more advanced student, these reveal the secret of joke telling, wordsplay understanding and chitchat on quotidian topics like sports, religiosity and pharmacology. Also pronunciation, gesticulation and skill augmentation.

Where from this book?

The Happy Phrase series of publications does not spring like a fat infant from the foreheads of its authors. A vast team of midwives is also in situ. We can't name them all of course, as most are anonymous third world printing plant workers, but here are some of our happiest phraseurs:

LIONEL OGILVY FROBISHER M.Theol (Cantab), Phil.D.Litt (Oxon) DSO CBE. The English tongue is Lionel Frobisher's mistress and tongue it he has, in language schools from Scapa Flow to the subcontinent. But for every mistress there is a wife, and Lionel's wife is boys. He has composed almost 30 volumes devoted to the education, training and enhancement of boys and their growth—many not published in this country. His most popular volume remains an encomia on young persons and smoking *How to Get Boys to Give It Up*. An enthusiastic nature walker he regularly holidays in the lush hinterlands of Morocco, Cambodia and Amsterdam.

WAYNE JOHN KANE A lexicographer with contributions to more than a dozen major dictionaries, Kane has authored monographs and articles on topics including the dative, the gerund and the great vowel shift. He is currently researching the devolution of the tripthong, the conditional of the subjunctive and Basque. He can be contacted via the Ararat Prison Hospital for the Criminally Insane.

DR MISS ELSIE SCRATCHWELL Dip.Cert. D.Litt (Bucks & Herts). The author of the only concordance to the Middle English epic *Piers Plowman* to be written in Old English, Miss Scratchwell has acquired a reputation as one of the most exacting, persistent and dogged editrixes among her many, many former colleagues of whom there are many. Her other works include *Living with Migraine*, *The Joy of Cats*, and *Cats Do Get Migraines*.

DR WARWICK PETROULIS PhD (University of Technology, Hobart). Author of the definitive study *Marriott/Sade: Deconstruction/Hospitality*, Petroulis believes that Derrida's notion that there is no relationship between word and thing can be applied to the foreign phrase book and his *Spanish for Emergencies* was a best-seller until withdrawn by order of the International Criminal Court.

1. Getting Started

 English is not a complex, complicated, arcane, convoluted, recondite or abstruse language but rather is renowned and distinguished for its simplicity, forthrightness and absence of bedecking embellishments. To accelerate the advent of fluency, self-repeat the following Happy Phrases in the quiet at home. If the household is not pacific, go elsewhere. In good time, over and over, your memory will be affected. Almost without heed, your native hesitation will be supplanted by an easy English.

Solo Practice—Lesson I

- I have twenty-eight.
- Behold the spatula, splendid utensil.
- Death and despair are man's boon companions.
- My niece is a spam-filter guru.
- Thank you. I have been honing it.
- I am not an American.

Solo Practice—Lesson II

- Do you smock?
- This tastes of freon.
- To be candid, not all of my cousins are actuaries.
- Please increase the dosage.
- I tell you I am not an American.
- Have the porter fetch a mallard.

Self Conversation—Dialogue I

- He enjoys boating. She enjoys it also. Their son is strange and does not enjoy boating.

- We like tennis. Are there any courts nearby? The human intestine is more than two kilometres in length.

- The cathedral is impressive. Your thin white shirt is taut across your nipples. Is the apse open to visitors?

- This restaurant was favoured by the town's writers and artists. Look, Japanese aircraft are strafing us. It is Pearl Harbor all over again.

Self Conversation—Dialogue II

- We are having lunch in the old town. My husband tried to kill me when I asked for a divorce. See, there are marks on my neck.

- Is your accent American? The soil here is mainly alluvial. I hail originally from Saskatchewan. It is in Canada. The reddish-brown pigmentation is due to a high concentration of phosphates in the ground water. Canada is not America.

- That very evening an opportunity occurred for Rob to win glory in the eyes of his new friends. She is adverse to rhubarb. These tissues are damp.

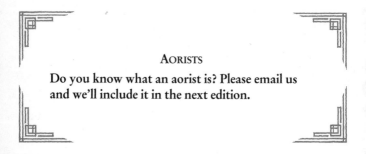

AORISTS

Do you know what an aorist is? Please email us and we'll include it in the next edition.

HOW TO SPEAK

As a phonetic language, English pronunciation is expeditiously achieved with adroit facility. For the not-native speaker, a small previous practice is advisable before attempting to deploy the appended phrases.

ACCENTS AND INFLEXIONS – as much as possible, English should be done without stress. If there is a hyphen, a small amount of pressure can be applied. You may, if you wish, change position. As to variations in accentuation, many are the adherents. When considering diacritical marks, such as the cedilla and the cummerbund, these are unemployed in workaday English. The umlaut, while not strictly required, is sometimes useful. We recommend keeping a handful in the pockets at all times.

POSITION OF MOUTH – when speaking, the mouth should remain approximately mid-way between the nose and the chin. The lips should never be more than 5 centimetres from the teeth. Ditto the tongue. Please Note: No attempt should be made to speak English in a vacuum.

THE APOSTROPHE – sometimes known as 'the Devil's cup hook', the apostrophe is rarely sounded. A sharp click, it is made by pressing the tongue against the roof of the mouse. If a mouse is not available, a small rat may be substituted.

THE CATASTROPHE – like the apostrophe, the catastrophe is not mentioned in polite conversation. It can, however, be simulated by clutching one's throat with both hands and emitting the sound of strangulation.

2. The World is Your English-Speaking Oyster

Be it the workaday necessaries of business or the hanker for adventure, wherever the lust of wander transports you, a smattering of English eases the passage.

By air, by land, by sea, across rivers and torturing mountain passes, you will never be lost in transit thanks to a handful of applicable English. Whether salty old tar or delightfully girlish flight attendant, your international conductor will find you easier of assistance if English is mutual.

At the foreign currency desk

- May I back-invoice you?

- Oranges are not the only fruit. Take the whortleberry, for example.

- Are you not sleepy? Even a little?.

While waiting for the ferry boat

- My lanyard is entangled in your bollards.

- They say the bosun is a Capricorn.

- Flotsam is as flotsam does.

When meeting the people smuggler

- Our ancestral hamlet has been laid waste.

- How much is that in piastres?

- You have lovely ankles.

On the discount airline

- Your fuselage is most commodious.

- My wife prefers a moustache.

- I am not an American.

- Look, an albatross!

Inside the shipping container

- My daughter has a tawny pippet. Its leg has gone numb.

- Do you have any magnets?

- I once took a turn with Nijinsky.

BRAND NAMES

Many common words in English were once the names of brands of products that became so popular as to be general. Well-known examples are *cellophane*, *velcro* and *Toyota Camry*. But did you know that these words were once brands?

Bread: The popular wheat-based product was first marketed by Kevin and Valerie Bread in the 1920s. A canny marketing campaign then presented 'Bread's foodstuff'—as it was officially called—as a staple food with an ancient history. Prior to its introduction, a 'sandwich' was simply a piece of meat or wodge of egg salad held tightly between the flat of two hands. Any memory older readers may have of eating 'Bread's foodstuff' before the First World War is simply a testament to the power of advertising or a symptom of neurological decline.

Walking: Septimus Walker introduced the now popular form of exercise—a contraction of *walkering*—in the 1820s. Prior to this people did not move, and simply passed each other things they wanted. When travelling they would fling their bodies from one position to the next.

Mollification: The emotional and social process of persuading someone to take a calmer and more forgiving attitude to a person or thing was developed by Melbourne music promoter Ian 'Molly' Meldrum in a series of workshops in the 1970s. He receives 7c in royalties every time the act is performed.

3. Making new friends

 Go wherever you will, a Happy Phrase melts the ice. Cordiality blossoms. Warm impressions become mutual. Fellow-feeling abounds. He might be a taxi driver. Perhaps she is your business confederate. Or your cell mate. Soon there will be more to it.

At the customs post

- Our coracle is awash.

- Please feel free to scrutinise this reticule.

- Try some of the lichen.

- May I touch your coiffure?

While waiting in line at the Sea World cafeteria

- No, I don't find your avuncularity presumptous.

- The generalissimo sure has an extensive entourage.

- For all their rough bravado, I find the leathernecks quite charming.

- I am not an American.

HOW TO GAG IN ENGLISH

English speakers love to kid with mirth. Here is one of a kind named 'A Shagging Dog Story'. Recount it to all and sundry if bursting sides are your desire.

A man was travelling abroad in a small red car. One day he left the car and went shopping. When he came back, its roof was badly damaged. Some boys told him that an elephant had damaged it. The man did not believe them, but they took him to a circus which was near there. The owner of the elephant said, 'I am very sorry! My elephant has a big, round, red chair. He thought that your car was his chair, and he sat on it!' Then he gave the man a letter, in which he said that he was sorry and that he would pay for all the damage. When the man got back to his own country, the customs officers would not believe his story. They said, 'You sold your new car while you were abroad and bought this old one!' It was only when the man showed them the letter from the circus man that they believed him.

In Sioux City, Iowa

- We are here for the coronation.

- Numismatics is her only true passion. Above all, the picayune.

- I have come a cropper.

- Hand me that tortoise.

mens rea: a giant bird, available to male Roman citizens (Lat.)

estoppel: an unshaven witness (Spanish)

prima facie: during testimony, getting a big sloppy kiss from well known Latin American band leader Louis Prima (rare)

modus operandi: name of a third rate graphic design firm, probably.

During High Mass

- Your flapjacks are legendary.

- The chancellor is a fellow collector. Lepidoptera, I think.

- Slithering through the brilliant undergrowth, the boa constrictor is symbolic of Africa's capacity to resist the siren call of undifferentiated modernisation. You have lovely ankles.

Eventually it will be necessary to inform someone that two other people are engaged in the act of public foreplay, and you will be faced with a decision about whether to employ the word 'canoodling'. This is probably the most important decision you will have to make in your life. Once known as someone-who-has used-the-word-canoodling the course of your future is set and necessarily involves permanent jauntiness, a dimpled smile, tubbiness and the wearing of floral print dresses even though your barren soul yawns like a black wound above the abyss, crying for consolation.

So think carefully.

4. Compliments, Affirmations and Endorsements

Butter them up, as the old saying says. Succour your interlocutor with these euphonious utterances. Thickly lay it on.

In Tashkent

- Yes, it is indeed a very fine expressway. Few speak ill of it.

- Your quinces are refreshing.

- I also like to wear my clothes very tight.

ENGLISH EXPORTS

English has given words to many other languages. In France they talk about le weekend and savoir-faire. Germans say 'gesundheit' and the Finns enjoy a 'sauna'. Whatever culture you are from whether you enjoy ravioli (an English word) or live in Beijing (an English word), English has been there first and your way of life has no authenticity whatsoever.

After intercourse

- Your bibelots are stunning.

- It smacks of latent modernism.

- Unfortunately, my canasta was a little rusty.

- That budgerigar has begun to moult.

When being introduced to a Mormon

- Your ligatures are superbly executed.

- My family takes the view that Lee van Cleef is very underrated.

- Come, let us take our liebfraumilch onto the patio.

- Go ahead. Frisk me.

Under fire

- What a terrific screen-saver.

- Assure the colonel that I shall apply myself assiduously.

- My mother always had a soft spot for abstraction. Pollock, in particular. Rothko, even.

- I love your bandanna.

5. Getting Bedded

For some, it is the luxury of a hot-water motel. For others, it is a rude couch beneath the stars. Either way, the securing of a place to lay the head will be an immediate necessity for the visitor, be it long of duration or for only a quick one.

Numerous matters will needs be discussed with your host. Facilities, charges, provisions, breakages, plumbing and furnishings will be touched upon. The following phrases are bound to elicit hospitable sentiments.

Without a confirmed reservation

- I'd rather be in Invercargill.

- Do all your rooms overlook the chemical works?

- We prefer the linoleum.

- This luncheon meat is speckled.

At the camping ground

- Is your downstairs ventilated?

- He is a timpanists' timpanist. The conductor of the San Diego Philharmonic will attest it.

- My dreams are flotsam on time's uncaring sea. Your skull grins through your face. What time is breakfast served?

- We have no fungible assets.

COMPOUND TERMS

A compound is an idea or concept which has a single meaning but is made up of more than one word. There are many such expressions in English. For example, virtual reality, kiss of life, coalition of the willing, dog paddle, fuck off.

During the feast of St Bernard of Clairvaux

- We were accosted on the funicular by a testy albino.

- What is your opinion of Greer's hypothesis?

- These trousers are made of hemp.

At the finest hotel in Argyllshire

- Kindly demonstrate the bidet.

- Where can we get our spaniel wormed?

- Gracious, what a transgressive gouache.

- I thought it was yoghurt.

In the high roller suite at Caesar's Palace

- The aroma is redolent of humus.

- My wife is Dutch Reformed.

- Any prospect of whistling up some marzipan?

- Grandpa was a notorious trencherman.

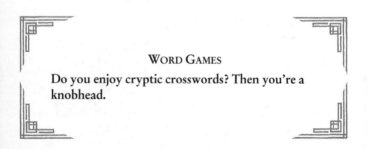

WORD GAMES

Do you enjoy cryptic crosswords? Then you're a knobhead.

THE LANGUAGE OF FLOWERS

In her classic account of Pacific Islander life *Coming of Age in Samoa*, Margaret Mead described the custom by which young Samoan girls wore a peony flower behind their left ear—which indicated that 'I am looking for a sweetheart'—or behind the right ear, which indicated that the wearer was affianced.

Subsequent researches have discovered that Mead made most of this up smashed on mai-tais in the Luau Bar of the Pago-Pago Hilton, and that no human society varies to any significant degree from contemporary Western life. Nevertheless, it has been estimated that an easy floral based system of sexual availability signalling would save more than 1.61 million annual wasted man-hours of sniff-testing jocks, eating vegetarian and seeing Meg Ryan movies with someone who just forgot to mention that she was practically engaged to that Mercedes salesman, for chrissake.

Ahem.

With this in mind we present the Mead flower system expanded for contemporary needs.

I am looking for a sweetheart

I am betrothed

Getting married in ten days and laid tonight

These wrist burns aren't a squash injury

I will come home with you, I will kiss you passionately and while you are filling the water bed I will take an overdose of your vitamin B tablets and call my steroid-abusing ex-boyfriend on your landline

I enjoy tennis

I am mad

I am currently having an affair with a married man, but he's going to leave his wife or wear a fern behind his ears. (As above)

A balcony above my head collapsed on my way out tonight. Also, I am looking for a sweetheart

6. Seeing Things

 Once lodged, curiosity supervenes. You seek to know the byways of local commerce. You pine to ken the customary behaviours thereabouts. Small purchases become necessary, or your appetite will brook no delay.

The moment has come to sally forth into the streets or fields, the highways and byways. But you have no fear. Equipped with the following indispensable English phrases, you will soon be enjoying free exchanges with similar others and having your needs fulfilled. And even, perhaps, fertilising the shoots of new friendship.

At the zoo

- Which way to the eland?

- The second mouflon looks a bit like Marcel Duchamp.

- You must have nerves of steel. Careful, it is excreting. Now your blouse is ruined.

- Is Doctor Baker still under Professor Schneider?

- The snark is chimerical.

From a hot-air balloon

- The sky is sober. A nameless dread grips my entrails.

- Look, a truant cassowary.

- The lavatory is entwined with lantana.

- He said he was West Indian. I told him to fuck off.

During a military putsch

- Our adjutant is the very figure of muscular Christianity.

- Did you bring the bisque?

- Mother thinks it smutty.

Recommended by your cousin Olaf

- The play of light entrances the senses. Kindly unfasten your corsets.

- It comes in twenty-three flavours. The compressor is out of order.

- Here, have a liquorice all-sort.

At the Volkswagen factory

- Excuse me, aren't you Lindt?

- I'm getting a repeated bang in the front
  mounting.

- The concatenation has been incessant.

- Are these promptings germane?

A WORD A DAY

Improve your vocabulary by using a new word a
day. Start with these:

    spongiform

    catflap

    flocculent

    papiloma

    ovo-alluvial

    bit

When you are confident with them, try them in a
sentence.

7. Provender and Beverage

Ravenousness comes to all. Ditto the periodic urge to tipple. So why endure famishment or desiccation for want of ordering capacity? A small bite in the hand, a hearty titbit or a quenching draught of the costliest liqueur—whatever your appetite commands, it will be satisfied when the following useful phrases are your companions of the table.

At the tapas bar

- Nonpareil jaffles.

- This place is chock full of atmosphere.

- They laughed at Gandhi. They laughed at Napoleon. Is your bottom itchy, too?

- Easy on the jerky, rabbi.

In the Savoy Grill

- More mulligatawny, grandmother?

- For heaven's sake, stop monkeying with the condiments.

- Waiter, there is a caterpillar in my chablis.

- Say, let's go back to my room for a nightcap!

If on the Atkins

- Luckily, I have extra albumen in my portmanteau.

- My paramour thinks it's natural.

- Roughage?

When challenged to eat a whole paella

- While you're there, try to inveigle some detergent.

- Your gifts are fists and curses. I have grown bitter with your love and sweet with your hatred.

- She made her name in chic-lit.

- The gorgonzola is on the credenza.

HOW TO CONNOISSEUR

Recently an appreciation of the French way of life has become more popular in the English-speaking world, due to a greater understanding of the benefits of multicul-turalism and also increased recognition of how shit English stuff is. *Vive le Republique* we all say, and in that spirit you will have to know all things French, such as giving a lady oral relief and collaboration. Also wine. No longer need the tasting of wine be a mystery. By mixing and matching the following handy phrases, rest assured of appearing knowledgeable, whether partaking in the most casual of sipping or the focused slurping of the gourmand. It is a...

fruity	drop	hint of tannin
assertive	vintage	touch of vanilla
velvet	snifter	aftertaste of ginger
smoky	cutting	bottom of pineapple
contumelious	press	bouquet of pomegranate

	little		**with a**
robust	example		gargle of crabmeat
draconian	nectar		fanfare of gemutlich
pensive	boisson		perfume of futility
chocolatey	cleanser		tincture of simony
vindictive	juice		snaplock of breasts
Episcopalian	potion		yesness of no
shapely	elixir		cape of invisibility
bladdering	asses' milk		odour of dead bear
raisinesque	mouthwash		means, motive and opportunity
shithouse	sherbet		body that won't quit
textural	punch		orangeness of applery
lead-contaminated	squeeze		phrase to come
spankworthy	hairy ball-sweat		drop of fruitiness
grape-flavoured	wine		flavour of grape

TECHNICAL MUSICAL TERMS: WHAT DO THEY MEAN?

sfumato: not sure

rallentado: um....

rubato: you got me.

8. Getting a Purchase

Be it a daily necessity or reminiscent gift, you must transact. For most, the supermarket suffices. For that peculiar thing, you need a privy vendor. Whatever satisfaction you seek in bazaar or boutique, at the gentleman's equipage emporium or the purveyor of a lady's specialities, be succoured by these English. Negotiation fluency ensures a rapid good buy. Make shopping a pleasure experience for buyer and seller alike.

Older readers accustomed to handling money will remember talk of 'monkeys' 'lobsters' and 'rhinos'. They are a mammal, a crustacean and another mammal respectively.

At the flea market

- These lederhosen are a tad snug.

- May I have an anaesthetic?

- I give not a fig for your filthy spondulicks.

- His daughter wants an aqueduct.

When selecting a terrapin

- Do you have one in mauve?

- According to Bourdain, the cloaca should still be flexible.

- A prelate never lies. A feminised landscape is traversed, mapped, contained. An army marches on its stomach.

At the contemporary furniture fair

- This one is sticky.

- My friend is a yuppie. She is motivated by an underlying competitiveness. How much for the non-irritant depilatory cream?

- Hey! Funky castors!

Ordering kibble over the phone

- I was assured that it glows in the dark.

- There, see. Surplus value is produced.
  Marx was right.

- It happened when I bingled my moped.

- What is kibble?

THE SUBJUNCTIVE FAMILIAR

Absolutely essential. Working as, for example, a
waiter you would need to say 'thou mayest likeste
chips' in cases where the chips' liking of would
eventuate in an indicative state only if a qualifying
indicative potential would be rendered actual by
the acceptance of the latter potential indicative.
(This is available on a laminated card.)

9. Culture Exchange

 A painting is silent. The bassoon has no tongue. Yet, by paradox, culture dialogue is heard everywhere in audience appreciation and disputation after it has been seen and absorbed. A cultivated conversation is sought. Unsophistication threatens embarrassment. English snippets give vent to sublime sentiment.

At the Stanley Kubrick retrospective

- The projectionist has been wait-listed for a same-sex knee-trembler.

- I, too, am a deep-focus aficionado.

- Show me your lasso.

- The key grip is something of a gadfly.

On the acceptance of your gay-niche novel by Faber & Faber

- The style guide suggests 'aboriginal'.

- The gusset is pure polyester. With this tiny chronometer strapped to my wrist, I will never be at a loss for the time. The buttons are made from casein.

- Will the ballyhoo be tax deductable?

- Mitch Miller.

HOW TO GERMAN

Many *Happy Phrase* readers would
like to learn to speak yet another
language. But this is not easy as there
are word lists, grammar rules and it is
necessary to wear, around the pelvis,
the apparatus. Luckily the Happy
Phrase team have developed a simple
module for developing alter-lingiustic
competency in a variety of other
parlances in this case the Teutonic
languages, while only knowing
English.

STEP 1: Add 'kyihk'—spelt 'chk'
twice to every sentence. It does not
matter where. The sound is derived
by remembering what it was like to
take cod liver oil while having a
head cold.
EXAMPLE: I am going to the market
with my friend and her sister to buy
some apples

GERMAN: *Ichk am going to the market with my friend and herchk sister to buy some apples*

STEP 2: change all 'a's to 'u's, 't's to 'd's, 'w's to 'v's and 's's to 'z's
Ich um going do der market vith my freund unde herch zizter do buy zum upplenz

STEP 3: add 'n' to any exposed vowel endings, and 'k' to any soft consonants

Ich um goink do der marketk vith myn freund unden herk zizter do buyn zum upplenzk

STEP 4: add be- to the front of any verbs and then move them to the end of the sentence
Ich um do der marketk vith mein freund under herk zizter zum upplenzk begoingenk bebuyenk.

Congratulations! This modular tongue works for four Teutonic languages with some minor adjustments:

FOR GERMAN: Sentences should be said in a full and open-mouthed fashion sounded well to the front of the face consistent with being heard above the sound of tanks advancing remorselessly eastwards.

FOR DUTCH: For men: A higher register and a greater emphasis on the 'e' can be gained by pretending you are ejaculating.
For women: that you have cystitis.

FOR SWEDISH: since forty per cent of all utterances in Swedish are spoken while ejaculating, the up-and-down register of the Scandinavian tongues can be attained by getting into the mindset of the situation in which the other sixty per cent of Swedish utterances are spoken, ruminating on the reasons for your impending suicide to a rural priest who has lost his faith in God played by Max Von Sydow.

FOR NORWEGIAN: who cares, but pretend the herring is rotting.

When applying for the artistic directorship of a contemporary dance company

- Her massing is not flattered by the chemise.

- No it is not endogenous. It is in fact exogenous.

- A rudimentary examination suggests cantilevering.

- You have pretty ankles.

- Very pretty.

When being presented with a medal at the Highland Games

- Bring me an effigy of Rod Stewart.

- Your antlers are incredible.

- She is pursuing a career in encephalography.

- Do you no ken the camber of my caber?

After a performance of *La Traviata* by inmates of the Louisiana State Penitentiary

- The choreographer's organza furbelows left us speechless.

- To tell the truth, I'm not really comfortable in the spotlight.

- It's like a bilberry, but more tart.

- Congratulations! You got triplets.

HOW TO GAG IN ENGLISH (2)

Very popular in English is the joke called a 'Knock, knock'. The jokester pretends to be a visitor who arrives with peremptory banging. A dialogue ensues.

Example A

Knock, knock.
   Who is there?
I am selling brushes.
   What kind of brushes?
They have bristles.

Example B

Knock, knock.
   Who is there?
Isobel.
   I don't know anybody called Isobel.
   Who are you really?
A brush salesman.
   I don't want any brushes.
Okay.

10. Doing your business

A happy phrase is the proven lubricant for input of fast-track feedback. At the international conference, your delivery will be English, similarly the sharing of warm relations with an end-user or two and negotiating it. Implement these phrases to enhance quality bottom linings.

NOUN CASES

Contrary to some guides, English has a wide variety of inflected noun cases which you must learn. They include the ablative, locative, vocative, palliative, rotative, dodecahesive, closeshavative, Raelian, homunculus, birdynumnum and genitive. (This is available as a stick-on tattoo.)

Ordering office supplies

- Will my performance indicators be negatively impacted?

- Your commitment to optimal outcomes cannot be impugned.

- Freemasons have abducted my houseboy.

- Terminate! Terminate!

- Would you like to come up to my room for a nightcap?

At the sperm bank

- By coincidence, Hot Gossip is my favourite group too.

- This eiderdown is besmirched with sauerkraut.

- Help! My houseboat is listing.

- I prefer to squeeze my own.

- Allegro. Fortissimo. Prego.

During a plenary session of the International Whaling Commission

- Is that a plankton in your pocket?

- See if you can't lay your hands on some bladder-wrack.

- In matters of the heart, I am a unilateralist.

- Their side insists on a doughnut-shaped table.

- We could go back to your room if you prefer.

At the Hollywood pitch meeting

- The protagonist is a regular dude.

- What we have in mind is a bedizened trollop.

- He wears upon his head the horns of a cuckold.

- Mozart is acceptable.

- Bruckheimer's scenario is trite.

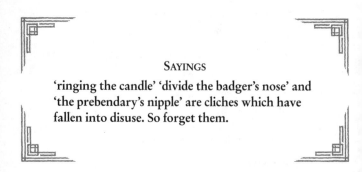

Sayings

'ringing the candle' 'divide the badger's nose' and 'the prebendary's nipple' are cliches which have fallen into disuse. So forget them.

HOW TO HIP-HAPPEN

Be cool, my man. And whether rappin' in the hood or just chillin' in yo crib, earn maximum respect with these hip 'in-crowd' phrases.

I am the walrus.

It's fun to stay at the YMCA.

Can you hear the drums, Fernando?

Up, up and away in my beautiful balloon.

What's new pussycat? Woah-oh-woah-oh-woah-oh.

Advances in the science of munitions and the increased use of mobile phones in petrol station forecourts have made necessary the development of a language for non-auditory persons lacking upper body limbs. PLATES (Provisional Language Assisting Tragically Eviscerated Subjects) requires the signer to twist on their back and point upwards as per breakdancing. It also requires two people.

11. Talk Lovely to Me

 Attraction to a stranger beckons but without flirt capacity in English, only the solitary remains. To win romance, a plenitude of sweet nothing must get into the lusted one's ear. Let consensual phrases scratch your ardorous itch. When a pillow talks to the affectionate heart, a happy phrase is the key.

HOW TO COURT

It has long been the practice of Anglophone lotharios to inveigle a winsome young filly (as the current 'slang' has it) to his lodgings with an invitation to 'come up and see my etchings', the purpose being not art appreciation but the stealing of a girl's virtue, in the unlikely event that a lass travelling independently should still possess it. 'Come and see my lithographs', by contrast is simply an innocuous invitation to inspect some cultural artefacts, so it is vital to distinguish them, although come to think of it I may have them the wrong way round.

Anyway, the following phrases are commonly heard variations on the above theme:

Would you like to come up and see my drypoints?

I have been impotent lately and hoped you would be the one to break the run.

Would you like to come up and see my gouache?

Do you have any experience in changing surgical dressings?

Would you like to come up and handle my miniature Brancusi?

Don't say you weren't warned about potential disappointment.

Would you like to come up and see my Ken Done?

You better love Kenny G and Malibu shooters or this will be a long night.

**Would you like to come up and see
how I have brought out the deco
quality of the original apartment?**

I am an obvious homosexual; you're
wasting your time.

I have a bright pink Warhol.

You into really kinky shit too?

**Would you like to come up and see
my Drover's Wife?**

Would you like to come up and see
my drover's wife.

At the unisex hairdresser

- Your yashmak is divine.

- Does this beverage contain lard?

- It is not so much a futon as a palliasse.

- Deploy the moving parts. See how smoothly they function.

During induction into the Coldstream Guards

- The major's batman is a veritable juggernaut.

- Yes, I would like a bigger unit.

- Drop those gooseberries, buster.

- Ours is the table with the small vase of edelweiss.

Every language contains phatic terms. These are words and phrases which have no meaning in themselves, but which can be inserted anywhere. Examples are *alors* in French, *caramba* in Spanish, and *would you care for something to eat?* in Russian. English has a stock of phatic phrases that is growing all the time, *tiens*. Here are some of the most popular new ones:

perhaps apocryphally

need for a royal commission

in a post 9/11 world

do you require counselling

the problem of childhood obesity

self-regulated industry

a good suburb to buy in

when you have children you'll know

While car pooling

- Can you smell kerosene?

- I am in a position to donate a bushel of cantaloupe.

- Would you—please don't do that—like to—careful of the architrave.

- By all accounts, her Thai is improving daily.

If stranded on a desert isle with an amorous sailor

- Look, cirrocumulus!

- Perhaps the Smurf costumes were an error of judgment.

- You'll find me less stentorian on the morrow.

- This toucan has been surgically augmented.

Words like 'heretofore' and 'nevertheless' are on the rise in English. Here's some new ones:

butforthis

neitheryetresolving

notminibarchargeincluding

neverBarbaraafterthatcasserolesupplyingup-onagainrelying

forbutnowfor

wubbledup

12. Stolen Moments

 The hurly-burly sub-sides. Quiet arrives. Your thoughts turn inside. Good luck for you as English is unsurpassed for inner self-meditation. Just mention these phrases to yourself in the slow emptiness of your head.

While contemplating the cosmic void

- This tuxedo is rented.

- Look, a plagiarist!

- I am not an American.

- It is my glands.

In the presence of the Maharishi Mahesh Yogi

- Is it still in escrow?

- Bestrew the bestiary with bergamot.
  Bestrew the bestiary with bergamot.

- The Europeans are working on a cure.

- I am the little red rooster.

A simple rule:

You would use should when you should imply ought and you shouldn't use would in situations when oughting should be implied should would happen to be used anyway. Would should ought a would, should should be employed, you would ought with should. So therefore you should, to ought would, which would, should would be used.

(Soon to be a major motion picture starring Matt Damon.)

After three months in an ice cave

- Sociobiology stinks.

- A horse walked into a bar.

- She wore a scrimshaw toggle.

- My jodhpurs are still at the laundry.

While plucking up one's courage

- My tailor is rich. Your milliner is poor. His barber is comfortable.

- She had a lascivious demeanour.

- To think that an archbishopric once lay within my grasp.

PRONUNCIATION

Some English words are hard to pronounce. Here's a helping hand:

autochthonous

coagulant

passacaglia

acacia

catafalque

Don't thank us!

13. Mind that Body

Notwithstanding prophylaxis, you encounter a medical quandary. It is normal. An apothecary will suffice for discombobulations of the alimentary canal or a small surgery, pain with severity or even prosthetic limbs. But a rupture, profuse bleeding, mental shock induced by grenade explosion mean a visit to hospital. Or a doctor must be brought, or you to him, perhaps her. A dentist likewise. Emergency chiropody? Have you insurance? Many such questions will be asked. Or just keep hale with aerobics. Where English is spoken, you might drink the spigot water with impunity and be fit like a fiddle.

While being rolfed

- My effluvium is vermilion.

- He was suspiciously secretive about his perineum.

- It was hibernating on her trolley.

- I thought it was yoghurt.

Being fitted with new dentures

- But bid me and I shall play the cornet.

- Victoria Falls, which way?

- Just give it a belt with the spokeshave.

- Are the maidens taboo?

HOW TO GESTURE

Certain words are considered too offensive to be spoken out loud. These words, known in English as 'verboten' or 'taboo' can only be expressed by the use of gestures. The following is a partial list of such words, together with directions for the appropriate gesture. Care should be taken in their use, as a mistake may offend or provoke.

Ampersand — Both hands, open, are held palms-upward, arms outstretched. With fingers closed, they are rotated up and around, simultaneously arriving at a position anterior to the shoulders before being infibulated with a brisk cascading movement.

Bungle—The index finger of the right hand (or, in the case of a left-handed person, the left hand) touches the forehead above the opposing eye. The relative position of the hips remains intact, one on top of the other. A shake of the head adds emphasis.

Cashew—The chin is raised to the maximum possible elevation. With a slight rocking motion, as if striving to remember a half-forgotten tune, the shoes are removed, first one, then the other.

Debauch—The 'Y' hand moves forward, up and away from the body. The buttocks follow.

Image not available at this time.

Endorphins — The left foot, assuming the '5' position, swings loosely at the knee. Galoshes may be worn, but the emphasis is diminished.

Fracas — The right elbow insinuates itself into the breast pocket of the interlocutor. Meanwhile, the fingers of the left hand execute a brisk glissando on the closed lid of an upright piano. (Note: A harmonium may be substituted if no piano is available.)

Gerbil — With the fingers of the left hand curled downward in the 'C' position, the thumb of the right hand is inserted and withdrawn a number of times in rapid succession. The eyes pop open in amazement and there is a sharp, somewhat scandalised, intake of breath.

Harbinger — With the tongue forming a bulge in the right cheek, the 'Y' hand grabs an imaginary cord above the head and jerks it downwards in a rapid pumping motion.

Incommunicado — An invisible bottle is held firmly between the thighs and the interlocutor invited to withdraw the cork by means of alluring glances.

Kierkegaard — The knees are pressed together tightly and the pelvic muscles clenched repeatedly. The right hand assumes the 'W' position.

When buying cocaine from a stranger

- Come autumn, the foliage is splendid. Cough, please. The larch, the ash, the elm, the oak, the willow. Your sputum suggests pleurisy.

- Perhaps I should not have hocked my pantaloons.

- You have lovely ankles.

- No, really.

At the birthing class

- It is both form-fitting and figure-hugging.

- This hamster is a retard.

- My inamorata has a hankering for tripe.

- That is not urine.

International Aviation and Naval Phonetic Semaphore Alphabet

Some commonly asked questions

Golf, Charlie?

Whiskey, Papa?

Foxtrot, Oscar?

Tango, Juliet?

Hotel, Victor?

Bravo, Romeo, Bravo

HOW TO SLANG

Everyone knows the famous, tiresome, cockney rhyming slang with which the denizens of London's East End have made tolerable their poverty-stricken, shit-encrusted lives. But did you know that the Australian public's long standing love affair with modernist and experimental poetry has generated an argot all of its own. Try this in on the beach or in the bistro!

Slang	From	Meaning
apples	apples and pears	tyres
Brahms	Brahms and Liszt	flask
plates	plates of meat	tamarind
rubbity	rubbity-dub	humpty-dumpty
horse's	horse's hoof	cheese-grater
bag	bag of fruit	bag
frog	frog and toad	apples and pears

14. Recreations

Nature is beautiful and a panorama. Contemplate it with club or gun in hand, if sport inclines you. Enjoy companionship when you have a tramp amid bursting flowers and enbalmed breezes, or a frolic with snow white upon the earth.

Likewise, take your pleasure indoors.

Bird watching with the Prince of Wales

- A kind of delirium grips one.

- Oh dear, I appear to have winged the beater.

- Feel my poncho. It is typhoon-proof.

- Ptarmigan? Methinks not.

On a yacht in the San Tropez marina

- The skipper wants you to gut the smelt.

- Her flippers are vulcanised.

- Our sommellier is a dinar billionaire.

While dancing the tango with Johnny Depp

- Show me how to calculate the hypotenuse.

- A touch of whippet, perhaps? Two, three, four. Or a borzoi?

- The greater part of interdisciplinary dialogue is bunkum.

- Does my halitosis offend?

Having been dealt a straight flush

- I was collared at the seminary picnic.

- These tissues are damp.

- What an abstruse denouement!

- Notwithstanding her operation, grandma was invariably sprightly.

HOW TO SPORT FAN

Be you an avid player or mere spectator, sporty chit-chat is the way to mix it. Whatever your game, you are sure to score with one of these winning phrases.

Go, Badgers!

I have rarely seen a more adept disposal.

The referee has just made an unfair determination.

We shall crush them like tiny kittens.

That player lacks mettle.

Oh, jubilation.

Oh, woe.

The same thing happened in the '93 final.

At the dachshund farm

- Try to second-guess the chaperone.

- An inexplicable lassitude is endemic.

- Yes, but are they porcini?

- He designed Sputnik.

Skinny-dipping in the Trevi fountain

- Your diagnosis strikes me as perfunctory.

- Who scarfed the pralines?

- It is a souvenir of Basutoland.

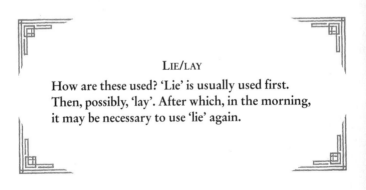

LIE/LAY

How are these used? 'Lie' is usually used first. Then, possibly, 'lay'. After which, in the morning, it may be necessary to use 'lie' again.

HOW TO GAG IN ENGLISH (3)

Riddles are very popular, particularly if they contain a sex reference, a pun or a conundrum. Here are some examples bound to raise a smile.

Q: When is a man not a man?

A: *If he is a pederast.*

Q: Has she got a nice pear?

A: *Yes, and her guava is attractive, too.*

Q: The man who works in the butcher shop is 190cm tall. He has red hair and wears size 11 shoes. What is his weight?

A: *Sausages.*

15. Ticklish Situations

Betimes, all goes not according to anticipation. Mischance befalls one and the moment is pregnant with blunder. A swift riposte will thwart misprision, offence, embarrassment, poor service, brandishment of weapons, adversity, detention, electro-genital torture. And lest memory abscond at a risky moment, seclude these phrases about your person for speedy deployment. Continuation of life may depend upon it, or the coming up of trumps in the end.

After accidentally farting in a crowded elevator

- An ocelot is ravaging our village.

- This one was taken by my niece. She took it when I still had sideburns. Would you like her telephone number? Her digital skills are unparalleled.

- I have an alibi.

metope: the quasi-pubic style of highly clipped goatee favoured by architects of the post bowtie generation.

spandrel: the type of architect who can produce a trilingual journal about post-neo-deconstructivist anti-building but can't put up a spice rack.

lesbian cymation: actually a wave-like frieze motif but it sounds icky, yeah?

Breaking up with your transgendered significant other

- As always, the problem is the flange.

- But you play a superb kazoo.

- An ambidexter is never unwelcome.

- I am a Presbyterian.

On failing to discover Weapons of Mass Destruction

- This soap will not lather.

- Allow me to explain transubstantiation. I can draw a diagram. Fetch a piece of charcoal.

- The muscatels are behind the terrarium.

- Look, geese!

Having just sneezed on the Pope

- That chasuble is gorgeous. Can you enhance the pixilation?

- I've never been much of a one for jazz ballet.

- You have pretty ankles.

- Our dramaturge has a wen.

16. Dealing with the Authorities

Rules are rules. Order must prevail. A permit is required. Wait here. Stand in line. Show your papers. Be quiet. Get undressed. Sign where indicated. Pay now. The organs of state must be obeyed. It is normal. All else is anarchy. Shut up.

If apprehended by border guards

- I, too, am a dog fancier.

- My aunt's wedding will be one of those New Age affairs. It is her second marriage.

- Nice webbing. Is it Prada?

- Khaki suits your complexion.

When applying for a licence to practise medicine

- Please accept this battery-powered device.

- It is sanctioned by Hindu tradition.

- Get those trousers down, you poltroon.

Under interrogation

- Are you alluding to my juvenilia?

- I was merely administering an emetic.

- It is an amalgam of a montage of collages.

- Ouch!

When pleading mitigation at your show trial

- The imam unexpectedly absconded.

- The colloquium was curtailed.

- Mother always maintained that it was a Stradivarius.

- I found something interesting when I googled your sister.

In the penitentiary

- This wickerwork is excellent.

- I am not an American.

- You have lovely ankles.

- May I borrow your lexicon?

INDEX

Conversations during Falconry

More than 150,000 copies in print, owing to a horrible miscommunication in the office. Everything you might ever think to say while engaging in this obscure mediaeval pastime. Includes a special appendix to assist people who may be attempting to purchase a yawl.
1 guinea, 32 pages recto verso.

Sex Chatter

A range of encomia and susurrations to impart during tender moments in the marital canopy or while having a tart. Special perforated and adhesive pages can be attached to the lover's forehead to assist in larding the beast with two backs with a discursive elan.
2 groats, elephant folio with endpapers.

Swahili for Beginners in Danish

For students of the Scandinavian tongue who may find themselves on the wrong steamer, due to a less than full command of the umlaut. Includes a section devoted to the tracing of lost skates in  Mombasa, and a special appendix to assist people who may be attempting to purchase a yawl. *A8 format, available by barter.*

Wrong French

For the independently wealthy traveller who doesn't need to give a snot about what the greasers think of him. A variety of professionally calibrated grammatical errors which will cause annoyance, confusion and even violence among our unwashed, collaboratively-minded amis. *£8.8.12.16.73.9.1/2 calf (the calf will only be offered for full cash payment).*

Jane's Yawl & Ketch Market

Includes a complimentary zoetrope and coupons for the acquisition of pemmican. *512 pages recto verso quando quando quando.*